The New Adventures of
MARY-KATE & ASHLEY ™

The Case Of The
Unicorn Mystery

Look for more great books in

⇒ The New Adventures of ⇒
MARY-KATE & ASHLEY™
series: ✓

The Case Of The
Unicorn Mystery

by Heather Alexander

HarperEntertainment
An Imprint of HarperCollins*Publishers*

A PARACHUTE PRESS BOOK

PARACHUTE PRESS
Parachute Publishing, L.L.C.
156 Fifth Avenue
New York, NY 10010

 **DUALSTAR PUBLICATIONS**
Dualstar Publications
1801 Century Park East
12th Floor
Los Angeles, CA 90067

HarperEntertainment

An Imprint of HarperCollins*Publishers*
10 East 53rd Street, New York, NY 10022

For information address HarperCollins Publishers Inc.,
10 East 53rd Street, New York, NY 10022.

ISBN 0-06-059596-5

First printing: March 2005
Printed in the United States of America

www.mary-kateandashley.com

10 9 8 7 6 5 4 3 2 1

A Real Unicorn

"**I** have a good one," I said to Ashley. We had been riding in our car for hours, and my sister and I were telling riddles. "What flower does everyone have on their face?" I asked.

"I give up," our mom said from the front seat.

Ashley twirled a piece of her blond hair and stared out the window. We passed another farm. We were way out in the country.

"Give up?" I asked.

"No way. I never give up," Ashley said, thinking hard. Then her blue eyes sparkled. "I've got it! Tulips! *Two lips*, right?"

"Right," I said. "Lindsay would like that riddle, don't you think?"

Ashley nodded.

Lindsay Munro is our good friend. Lindsay and her family moved out to the country a couple of years ago. Our mother was driving us to her house for a visit. We were going to watch her compete in the Flower Festival this weekend.

"Is Lindsay growing tulips again this year?" Mom asked.

"Yes," Ashley said. "She told me these tulips are even prettier than last year's."

"Wow! She won first place for her tulips last year," I said. "I guess she'll win again this year."

"I wonder what her secret is," Mom said. She turned on the windshield wipers. The sky had turned gray, and it had started to drizzle.

"I guess she has a super-green thumb," I joked. That's what people say when someone is good at gardening. I petted our dog, Clue, who was sleeping on the seat between me and my sister. Clue is a basset hound, and boy, does she snore loudly! "How much longer, Mom?"

"Mary-Kate! You just asked me that five minutes ago!" Mom said, laughing. "We're almost there."

"Stop the car! Stop the car!" Ashley suddenly screamed.

Mom hit the brakes, and the car stopped. "What's wrong?"

"Look! Over there. It's a . . . It's a unicorn!" Ashley cried.

"What?" I rolled down my window and peered into the foggy drizzle. Clue woke, and her ears pricked up.

"It *is* a unicorn! Mom, drive closer!" Ashley yelled.

Mom started driving slowly down the road. Then she stopped in front of a white unicorn.

"Oh." Ashley groaned. "It's not real."

A huge wooden sign in the shape of a unicorn stood in front of a fruit stand. It had large angel-like wings and a horn coming out of its forehead.

"Of course it's fake," I told Ashley. "Unicorns aren't real."

"Let's get out anyway," Mom said. "Those strawberries look good."

Mom clipped a leash onto Clue's collar and Ashley and I scrambled out of the car. The fruit stand was piled high with berries, peaches, and melons. Huge buckets overflowed with colorful flowers. An old man with curly white hair stood by a cash register.

"Welcome," he said. "My name is Bill. Let me know if you need any help."

Mom smiled at him and smelled the

strawberries. "Yum. Let's buy some for Lindsay's family." She gathered berries into a bag.

"Wow! You sure do like unicorns," Ashley said to Bill. She pointed to the little model unicorns that sat on the shelf by the cash register. There must have been more than twenty unicorns there.

"Everyone in this town loves unicorns," Bill said, his blue eyes twinkling. "Did you know that unicorns live in our hills?"

"Really?" Ashley said.

Bill nodded. "Our town is famous for them."

I laughed. Loudly.

"Mary-Kate!" Ashley whispered.

"Sorry," I said to Bill. I knew it was rude to laugh at someone. "But unicorns are made-up . . . pretend. Right?" I asked.

"Wrong," Bill said with a smile.

"Have you ever seen one?" I asked.

"Well, no. No one has—yet. The time

hasn't been right." Bill bent closer to us and whispered, "But it will be soon."

"What do you mean?" Ashley asked, leaning on the counter.

"The town legend says that unicorns can be seen during the month of June, but only if *three* rainbows have appeared in the sky that month," Bill said.

"Hey, it's June now!" I said.

Bill smiled. "And we've already had two rainbows this month. I've been waiting my whole life for three rainbows in June."

"I'd love to pet a unicorn," Ashley said. She had a faraway look in her eyes. "I think unicorns are beautiful."

"Even if we do get a third rainbow," Bill said, "you'll have to catch the unicorn first."

"Catch a unicorn?" I cried. "Isn't that like trying to catch Bigfoot? You can't catch something that's not real."

"Ah, but there *is* a way to catch a unicorn, if you believe in it." Bill pulled a small rolled-up paper tied with a purple ribbon out of a clay jar. He untied the ribbon and handed the paper to Ashley.

"This will tell you how to catch a unicorn," Bill said.

Ashley read the tiny writing out loud:

To capture the magical one-horned
    horse,
Follow exactly this special course.
Find the oldest tree in town,
And lay your presents upon the ground.

First, offer a tasty treat—
Something powdered, tart, and sweet.
Then leave a sparkly gift to wear,
A delicate rainbow for the hair.

Do this after the third rainbow in June,
And, behold, a unicorn shall appear
    soon.

"That is so cool," Ashley said.

"You can have it," Bill told her, as Mom paid him for the berries.

"Thanks!" Ashley said.

"Let's go, girls," Mom called. She and Clue headed toward the car.

"Why do you want that silly poem?" I asked Ashley.

"If there is a third rainbow while we're here, then I can try to catch a unicorn." Ashley's eyes shone with excitement.

Bill pulled a pink tulip from a bucket of flowers. He handed it to Ashley. "Unicorns love tulips. I hope this flower helps you find one."

"Thanks so much," she said.

I couldn't believe it. Ashley was always so logical. She liked to have all the facts. She liked things to make sense. So how could *she* believe in unicorns?

2

DID SOMEONE SAY *MYSTERY*?

As we drove over the winding roads, the sun began to peek through the clouds.

"Are we there yet?" I asked.

"Soon," Mom said. "Soon." She steered the car up a steep hill.

I leaned over to scratch Clue behind one ear. She loves that. I looked up just as we reached the top of the hill. I couldn't believe my eyes—the sky was filled with color.

"Wow!" Ashley and I said at the same

time. I had never seen a rainbow that bright and beautiful before.

"I wish I brought my camera," Mom said, heading the car down the hill. I saw a white house with blue shutters near the bottom. "That's Lindsay's house," Mom said.

"It's number three," Ashley said suddenly.

"What? Lindsay's house?" I asked.

"No. This is the *third* rainbow in June. Bill said that they already had two. This means a unicorn will appear soon," Ashley explained.

"Oh, Ash, come on—"

But I didn't get to finish, because a scream rang out. It was coming from Lindsay's house!

Mom pulled into the driveway.

"Oh, no! It's Lindsay," Ashley said. She pointed to one side of the house.

Lindsay stood there, her face buried in her hands. Her mother was holding her.

Mom turned off the car, and Ashley and I

raced over to our friend. Clue followed us.

"What happened? What's wrong?" I cried.

Lindsay looked up. Tears streamed down her cheeks, but her eyes brightened when she saw us. She stepped away from her mom and gave us each a big hug. "Oh, Mary-Kate . . . Ashley . . . I can't believe it happened again." Lindsay pointed toward the ground. "My tulips!"

Ashley and I gazed down and gasped. Lots of green stems were sticking out from the dark brown dirt—but none had a flower on top. A few red tulip petals lay on the wet ground.

"What happened to the tops of your tulips?" I asked her.

"I don't know," Lindsay said. Clue sniffed the dirt at her feet. "They looked great this morning. But when I came out after the rain stopped, all the flower heads had been destroyed!"

Ashley put an arm around Lindsay's

shoulders. "You said that it happened *again*. What do you mean?"

Lindsay nodded. "This is the second time this month that some of my tulips have been ruined."

"I don't understand," I said. "Why does this keep happening to your tulips?"

Lindsay pushed her chin-length brown hair out of her eyes, then shrugged. "I don't know. I've been working so hard, taking care of the tulips I'm growing for the Flower Festival. I really want to win again. *Everyone* knows that."

"Come inside, girls!" Lindsay's mom called.

I tied Clue on a long leash to a nearby cherry tree. Pale pink cherry blossoms covered the entire yard.

We all went inside, and Ashley and I brought our backpacks upstairs and unrolled our sleeping bags in Lindsay's bedroom. Then we hugged and kissed our mom good-bye. She would pick us up in two days, on Sunday night, after the Flower Festival.

The three of us ran out to the yard to play with Clue. Lindsay stopped when she saw her ruined tulips again. Her shoulders sagged. I hated to see Lindsay so sad.

"Don't worry," I said. "Your other tulips are amazing!" I pointed to the bright yellow tulips in the backyard.

Lindsay followed my gaze. "They are pretty, but I want to know what happened to these. It doesn't make sense."

"Why?" Ashley asked.

"The petals didn't come off by themselves. I think someone ripped them off," Lindsay said. "I can't figure it out. It's a mystery."

"Did you say *mystery*?" Ashley asked. She looked at me and smiled.

Ashley and I love a mystery. We're detectives. People call us the Trenchcoat Twins. At home we run the Olsen and Olsen Detective Agency out of the attic of our house.

"We could solve your mystery for you," I told Lindsay.

"No. You came here to have fun with me, not to work," Lindsay said.

"Solving mysteries *is* fun," Ashley said. "Right, Mary-Kate?"

"Right," I said. "The Trenchcoat Twins are on the case!"

"Thank you! Thank you!" Lindsay cried. "I hope you can find out who did this before the Flower Festival."

"Tell us about your tulips," Ashley said.

"I *had* four beds of tulips," Lindsay said.

"Tulips sleep in beds?" I asked. "Do they have blankets and pillows too?"

"No, silly!" Ashley said. "*Beds* are areas in a garden where flowers grow. Right?"

"Right," Lindsay said. "I have a pink tulip bed in the front yard. I have yellow tulips in the backyard. And I was growing red and white tulips, one bed on each side of the house. Last week the heads—that's the petal part—of my white tulips were all ripped off. And today the heads of my red ones are gone. The Flower Festival is in two days." Lindsay's forehead wrinkled with worry. "I hope the rest of my tulips will be okay."

"Let's take a close look at the scene of the crime—the side flower bed," Ashley said.

Lindsay and I followed her to the area. My sister and I got down on our hands and knees to examine the flowers.

Ashley pointed to a stem. "The stems are still here. Only the petals were pulled off."

"I don't see any footprints," I said, checking out the dirt. "But there sure are a lot of cherry blossoms on the ground." I peeled pale pink petals, still damp from the rain, off my sneakers.

"Our yard has the most cherry trees in

the area. Every spring the blossoms fall off the trees. Mom thinks it makes the ground look as if it's covered with cotton candy," Lindsay said.

"I don't see any clues here. Maybe the rain washed them away," I said. "Lindsay, is there anyone who would want to ruin your tulips?"

"Yes!" Lindsay said. "Carly Keller."

"Who is she?" Ashley asked.

"Carly lives down the road. She's in my fourth-grade class," Lindsay said. "Carly has to be the best at everything. In gym she tries to run faster than me. In spelling she tries to get more words right than I do. Even at lunch she makes sure she brings more chocolate-chip cookies than I do!"

If Carly always competed with Lindsay, that would give Carly a motive to destroy Lindsay's tulips. A *motive* is the reason someone commits a crime.

"Does Carly grow tulips too?" I asked.

"No. Carly is growing roses for the Flower Festival. But last week she came over to see my tulips," Lindsay said.

"Really?" Ashley asked. "Why?"

"I don't know," Lindsay said. "She looked at them for a long time. She asked me about the soil I use. And then she did the weirdest thing."

"What?" Ashley and I both asked.

"She took out her camera and snapped a picture of my tulips. She said she was taking nature pictures, but I didn't believe her," Lindsay said.

"Did Carly come by before or after your first bed of tulips was destroyed?" I asked. I knew the timing of events was very important when solving a mystery.

"One day before," Lindsay said.

"Do you think Carly did it?" Ashley asked me.

"Yes!" yelled a voice from high in the trees.

3

FLOWER POWER

We all looked up. Lindsay's eight-year-old sister, Abby, climbed down a wooden ladder nailed to the trunk of a tree. She had the same round face and dark brown eyes as Lindsay. Her shorts and T-shirt were damp and stuck to her skin.

"Abby, you're all wet! You should have come inside with Mom and me when it rained before," Lindsay said. She turned to us. "When she's not at her computer, Abby is almost always in her tree house."

"If I had come inside," Abby said, "I wouldn't have gotten such cool pictures of the rainbow." She pointed to a small digital camera hanging around her neck. "Hi, Mary-Kate! Hi, Ashley! I think Carly destroyed the tulips. She's been around our yard a lot lately. I saw her today from my tree house."

"You did?" Lindsay said. "What was she doing?"

"I'm not sure," Abby said. "I was busy taking pictures, and then I just saw her leaving our yard."

I turned to my sister. "I think we might have our first suspect."

"But we have no evidence to prove that it was Carly who ruined the flowers," Ashley said. *Evidence* is something that shows that someone was someplace or did something. She turned to Abby. "Do you remember when you saw Carly?" she asked. "Was it before or after it started raining?"

Abby shook her head. "I don't remember."

"We need to go talk to Carly and ask her some questions," I said to Abby and Lindsay.

"Let's go," Lindsay said, skipping across her wide lawn to the dirt road that led to Carly's house.

"Wait one second," Ashley said. She ran into the house. A few minutes later she came out with her backpack. All our detective supplies were inside: Ashley's detective notebook, a magnifying glass, and plastic evidence bags. Ashley always likes to be prepared.

Ashley, Lindsay, Abby, and I headed down the road. We left Clue behind to play with the Munros' dog, Goldie.

The sun was hot that afternoon. I pulled my baseball cap down lower to shade my eyes. Lindsay began to clip her hair back with a large barrette.

"Wow! Your barrette really sparkles in

the sun!" Ashley told Lindsay. "May I see it?"

I grinned as Lindsay handed Ashley her barrette. My sister loves fashion!

"Oh! The barrette is a glittery rainbow. I love it!" Ashley said.

"Did you see the rainbow today?" Abby asked.

"Yes!" Ashley said. "It was beautiful. And Bill, the man at the fruit stand, said it was the third rainbow in June. That means a unicorn will appear soon!"

"Everyone in our town is crazy about unicorns," Abby said. "I wish I could see a unicorn."

"Bill gave Ashley a tulip. He said unicorns love tulips," I said.

"I didn't know that," Abby said. "Hey, Lindsay, maybe a unicorn ate your tulips!"

"Ha-ha! Very funny!" Lindsay stuck her tongue out at her little sister. "Tell that to Nick. He'd love to write about it in *Nick's News*."

"Who's Nick?" I asked.

"Nick Martin is in our school, and *Nick's News* is his online mini-magazine. It has all the news in town. It's an extra-credit project," Lindsay explained. "Poor Nick. He really wants to get the highest grade in school, but our town is so boring that barely anyone reads his mini-mag."

"Here's today's copy." Abby pulled a few folded sheets of paper out of her shorts pocket. She handed it to me.

I opened it and looked at the headlines. FLOWER FESTIVAL COMES TO TOWN! FIRE TRUCK IS REPAIRED! WEATHER REPORT SAYS RAIN! Lindsay was right. It wasn't too exciting.

Ashley handed Lindsay back her barrette as we came upon a pretty farmhouse.

"There's Carly," Abby said, pointing.

A girl with long black braids was on a swing in the front yard. Rosebushes with the most amazing blossoms I had ever seen were planted by the swing set. Each petal was large and velvety. As we walked into the yard, I could smell the wonderful, sweet scent of the flowers.

"Hi, Lindsay and Abby!" Carly called as we headed toward her. "What's new?"

Lindsay stood by Carly's swing. "More of my tulips were destroyed today."

I watched Carly's face closely. She looked surprised. *Hmm*, I thought. *Maybe she's a good actress.*

"Really? That's horrible!" she said, but she didn't sound too upset. She glanced at her rosebushes. "I'm glad my roses are fine. Everyone says they're sure to win first prize in the rose competition."

"They do look nice," Lindsay said. "Carly, these are my friends Mary-Kate and Ashley."

"Hi!" Carly said. "Do you want to swing?"

"Sure," I said. Lindsay and I each sat on a swing. Ashley and Abby stood by a large oak tree.

As I swung, I looked over Carly's large yard. From up high it looked like a carpet of bright green.

"I can swing higher than you can," Carly told Lindsay. She began to pump her legs harder and harder.

Boy, Carly really is very competitive, I thought.

"You know what?" Carly said. "If my roses win the rose competition, I'll have *eight* first-place ribbons and trophies in my living room!" She smiled at Lindsay. "I have seven now. How many do you have, Lindsay?"

"Um . . . I won one at the Flower Festival last year. And I've won two for horseback riding, one for soccer, two for art, and one for jump roping," Lindsay said. "Seven."

"I should have more than seven, but I wasn't wearing my lucky sneakers the day of the jump-rope competition." Carly frowned. "So we're tied now, right?"

"I guess," Lindsay said. "It doesn't really matter, though."

"Yes, it does," Carly said, her eyes flashing. She swung higher and higher. "If I win the rose competition on Sunday and you lose the tulip competition, then I'll have more awards than you do!"

I rolled my eyes at Ashley. Carly was too much!

"I've only ever won *one* trophy," Abby said.

"What for?" I asked.

"Most Improved Hula Hooper!" Abby laughed. We all did too. It was a funny award.

"But it's okay that I've only won one award," Abby said. "There's no room on the living room shelf for any more awards. Lindsay's take up all the space."

Carly frowned. "My awards take up *more* space."

Suddenly Ashley's eyebrows shot up.

"Mary-Kate, could you come here?"

I slowed my swing and jumped off, as Carly and Lindsay swung higher and higher. I hurried to my sister's side.

"Watch Carly's feet," Ashley whispered to me.

I stared at Carly's white sneakers as her feet moved up and down. Then I saw it— stuck to the soles of her sneakers.

Wet cherry blossoms!

I looked around her yard. "There are no cherry trees here," I said to Ashley.

"Exactly," she said. "But there are lots of cherry trees in *Lindsay's* yard, and lots of wet cherry blossoms on the ground. That's evidence that Carly was in Lindsay's yard today . . . after it started raining—"

"Which is when the tulips were destroyed!" I added.

SOMEONE IN THE BED!

That night after dinner we all sat in the Munros' family room. Ashley pulled out her detective notebook and opened to a blank page. We discussed what to write.

SUSPECT #1: Carly Keller
MOTIVE: Wants more awards than Lindsay
EVIDENCE: Cherry blossoms on shoes

"Wait," I said. "I don't think that's enough evidence to say it's her for sure. Carly told us she was out taking nature photos all day, and that's how the cherry blossoms got onto her sneakers."

"I don't believe her," Lindsay said. "Abby said she saw Carly in our yard. Plus, Carly will do anything to beat me."

"She's still a good suspect," Ashley said to me. "Actually, she's our *only* suspect right now. Let's look for more clues tomorrow."

Woof! Woof! Woof!

I pulled my sleeping bag over my head. It was the middle of the night. Why was Clue barking? I tried to go back to sleep.

Woof! Woof!

I opened my eyes and peeked around Lindsay's dark room. Ashley was lying next to me in her sleeping bag. Her eyes were open too.

"What's going on?" she whispered.

I sat up and saw Clue by the window. She barked again.

Ashley and I hurried to the window. Lindsay got out of bed too. We pulled back her curtains and stared into the darkness.

There was a half-moon. In the pale moonlight I could see Lindsay's backyard.

Suddenly, Ashley grabbed my shoulder. "There's someone outside!" she said. "In the back tulip bed!"

I squinted into the darkness. It was hard to see. But then I saw a white figure moving around the flowers!

"Let's go!" Lindsay cried.

The three of us hurried out of her room and down the hall. We scrambled down the dark stairs.

"Quiet!" Ashley warned us.

We tiptoed into the kitchen and toward the back door.

Then we heard a noise—and froze.

We were not alone.

Someone was opening the back door.

Someone was coming into the kitchen!

5

A NEW SUSPECT

Suddenly the kitchen light flicked on. I squinted as bright light flooded the room.

"What are *you* doing here?" Lindsay cried.

We all stared at Abby. She stood by the light switch next to the open back door. She was wearing a short pale pink nightgown, and her brown hair was messy from sleep.

"Something was outside!" Abby said. "I heard it from my room, making noises in the garden. I opened the door to see what it was."

"What was it?" Ashley asked.

"I don't know," Abby said. "It ran off."

"I bet it was Carly," Lindsay said.

"Abby," Ashley said. "Why are your feet all dirty?"

The three of us stared at Abby's bare feet. They were covered with dirt.

"I stepped outside to take a picture of whatever was in the garden," Abby explained. She held up her camera.

"What in the world is going on here?"

We all turned to see Mr. Munro enter the kitchen. He wore a bathrobe and didn't look happy.

"We heard noises outside," Lindsay said. "It woke all of us up."

Lindsay's dad walked over to the back door, turned on the outside spotlight, and looked out. "Oh, no!" he cried.

Everyone crowded around him in the

doorway. Lindsay let out a shriek. All her yellow tulips in the back flower bed had been destroyed. The heads had been ripped off the flowers. Stray petals lay on the ground. Lindsay began to cry.

Abby hugged her.

Mr. Munro looked around the yard. "There's no one out there anymore." He stepped back into the kitchen and closed the door.

"Excuse me," I said to Mr. Munro. "Do you have a flashlight?"

"In the drawer," he said, pointing to a drawer near the sink. Ashley reached for the drawer handle. "Whoa! What are you girls doing?" Mr. Munro asked.

"We need to go out and collect clues while the crime scene is still fresh," Ashley explained.

"No way. Not tonight. It's three in the morning. Everyone is going back to bed," he said.

"But, Dad!" Lindsay cried. "Mary-Kate and Ashley are detectives!"

"And they'll still be detectives in the morning," Mr. Munro said. "No arguing."

I looked at Ashley and shrugged. Sometimes it's hard being a ten-year-old detective! I sure hoped that any clues would still be there when the sun rose.

Early the next morning the three of us hurried down the stairs and out the back door.

"Yuck!" Ashley cried as she stepped onto the grass. "It's all wet."

"Everything is wet," Lindsay said. "It must have rained last night after we went back to bed."

I pointed to the muddy flower bed. "I was hoping to find footprints of the culprit, but the rain washed away any evidence."

"Abby's feet were dirty last night," Ashley reminded me.

"I know," I said. "But we have no motive for her." I turned to Lindsay. "Do you think your sister would want to hurt your flowers?"

Lindsay shook her head. "No. Abby wants me to win."

Lindsay bent down to look at the tulips, and Ashley whispered to me, "I think we should list Abby as a suspect. She was outside last night when the flowers were destroyed."

Ashley and searched the backyard for clues. We checked every inch of grass but found nothing strange.

When we went back inside, Mrs. Munro was in the kitchen, stirring pancake batter. "Good morning, girls," she said. Then she looked at Lindsay's sad face. "Oh, honey, I'm so sorry about your tulips. Sometimes animals eat flowers, and there's nothing you can do about it. But don't worry—you still have one more bed of beautiful tulips."

"Animals?" Ashley turned to me. "We

never thought of that. Maybe the culprit is an animal. Maybe a groundhog or a deer."

"It could be," I agreed.

"I'm making your favorite chocolate-chip pancakes," Lindsay's mom said. "Go run upstairs and wash up. Try to get Abby off the computer so she can have breakfast too."

Lindsay turned to us. "Getting Abby away from her computer can be really hard. Maybe you two can do it."

We quickly washed up. The sweet smell of pancakes drifted upstairs. We poked our heads into Abby's room. She was at her desk, staring at her computer screen. Her digital camera was by her side.

"Hey," I said, suddenly remembering that Abby had her camera with her last night. Maybe she got a picture of the culprit! "May I see the pictures you took last night?" I asked her.

Abby turned toward us and shook her

head. "I didn't get any pictures. My battery was dead. Can you believe it?"

"Too bad." Ashley peeked at the screen. "If we had your photos, we could have seen who was near the tulips last night. All we know is that the person was wearing white."

"Or maybe it was a white animal, like my mom said," Lindsay pointed out.

I took a deep breath. I felt weird asking Lindsay's sister this question, but I knew I had to. "Abby, did you ruin the flowers last night?"

Abby looked totally shocked. "No way! Not me!"

"Okay, sorry," I said. I didn't want to make her feel bad.

"What are you reading?" Ashley asked Abby.

"*Nick's News.*" Abby turned the screen so we could all see. "Look at the new headline."

"'Unicorn Appears in Town!'" I read.

"A unicorn?" Ashley and Lindsay cried at once.

I read the article. It said that last night several people in town spotted a unicorn galloping through their yards.

"Do you think there really *is* a unicorn?" Ashley asked.

"No way," I said.

"There could be," Abby said. "Several people saw it."

"Mary-Kate!" Ashley said suddenly. "I think we have another suspect. Maybe a *unicorn* ate Lindsay's tulips!"

6

TIPTOE THROUGH
THE TULIPS

"**Y**ou think a unicorn did it?" I asked.

"Yes," Ashley said. She pulled out her detective notebook and started writing.

SUSPECT #3: Unicorn
MOTIVE: Loves tulips

I wasn't so sure. "What clues do we have?"

"First," Ashley said, "there were three rainbows in June. Second, a unicorn was spotted in town last night. Third, we saw something white in the flower bed last night."

Then she pulled a small piece of paper out of the back of her notebook. It was the unicorn poem from the fruit stand.

"That's so cool!" Abby cried. "I bet the unicorn is still here in town. We should try to find it."

"We don't have time to run around and look for a silly unicorn," I said to Ashley. "We have a mystery to solve, remember? The Flower Festival is tomorrow, and Lindsay only has one tulip bed left."

"But if it really was a unicorn that ruined the tulips," Ashley said, "this will help us catch it!"

I sighed. "This poem is like a big riddle." I read the poem out loud. "'To capture the magical one-horned horse, follow exactly this special course. Find the oldest tree in town, and lay your presents upon the ground.'"

Ashley turned to Lindsay. "Where's the oldest tree in your town?"

Lindsay wrinkled her nose as she thought. "I'm not sure."

"I know!" Abby cried. "There's that huge oak tree near Carly's house. There's a little sign at the bottom of the tree saying it's hundreds of years old!"

"But what about the two gifts we have to leave for the unicorn?" I asked. "It says 'First, offer a tasty treat—something powdered, tart, and sweet.'"

"Could it be a powdered doughnut?" Lindsay suggested.

"Not tart," Ashley said. "A lemon?"

"Not very sweet," I said.

"Or tasty," Abby added, making a face.

"What about the second thing we need to leave?" Ashley asked. "The poem says 'Then leave a sparkly gift to wear, a delicate rainbow for the hair.'"

"How do you put a rainbow into hair?" Abby asked.

"Maybe it's colored ribbons to braid

through the unicorn's mane," Ashley guessed.

We made a lot of guesses, but nothing seemed quite right again. We would have to keep thinking.

"I say we go back to Carly's house and ask her some more questions," I said. "She's our best suspect. I mean, there's a bigger chance that *she* did this than a *unicorn*!"

Everyone agreed.

Later that morning Ashley, Lindsay, and I walked up the road to Carly's house. Abby stayed home to finish some schoolwork. On the way we found the huge old oak tree. It was enormous!

"Now we just have to figure out the part of the riddle that tells us what two things to leave," Ashley said.

"What are you girls doing here?" a voice called out.

We turned and found a boy our age staring at us. He had large round glasses and curly blond hair. He held a notebook and pencil in his hands.

"Nick!" Lindsay said. "We were taking a walk. These are my friends Mary-Kate and Ashley. What are you doing?"

"Looking for stories for my next issue of *Nick's News*," he said.

"Is there really a unicorn?" Ashley asked.

"That's what people are saying, so that's what I'm reporting." He smiled. "More people looked at my Web site this morning than ever before. Everyone wants to know about the unicorn. If I can find more evidence of the unicorn, I'll be sure to get the highest grade for my site."

He turned to Lindsay. "What happened to your tulips last night? I heard more were destroyed."

Lindsay frowned. "Yes. All the heads were ripped from the stems—again."

Nick took notes. "Do you know who did it?"

"No," Lindsay said.

"I think I'll take a picture of your destroyed tulips for my next issue. 'Too Late for Tulips' will be my headline. I have to go photograph the news!" Nick said, and rushed off.

We watched him run down the road. "That was strange," I said.

"That's what I was thinking too," Ashley said. "If the flowers were ruined only last night, how did Nick know about it already?"

"Do you think Nick did it?" I asked.

"I don't know," Ashley said. "But we should keep an eye on him. Let's go see Carly."

Her yard was empty when we entered her front gate.

"Hello? Carly?" Lindsay called.

Carly jogged toward us from one side of her house. She looked as if she had been caring for her flowers. Her gardening gloves and the knees of her jeans were covered with wet soil. She held a watering can that dripped as she ran.

"Hi." Carly smiled at us. "I'm glad you came back. I've spent all morning with my roses. They are so beautiful this year, aren't they?" She pointed at the bright red flowers on their thorny stems.

"They sure are," Ashley said. "They're bigger than any roses I've ever seen!"

Carly smiled. "I know."

Lindsay went to look closely at the flowers with Carly. I looked at Carly, then at the rosebushes. Something didn't make sense.

"Ashley," I whispered. "Look at the rosebushes. The soil around them is dry and untouched."

"But Carly has a watering can and is covered with wet dirt," Ashley said. "She wasn't taking care of those roses. What's going on?"

"Are you coming back, Carly?" a boy's

voice called out from the side of the house.

Carly pretended not to hear. She bent over to smell her roses.

"Carly!" the boy yelled. "I'm not weeding for you anymore!"

Lindsay stepped forward. "Carly, your brother is calling you."

Carly laughed. "It—uh—doesn't matter."

I looked at Ashley. Carly's laugh had sounded very fake. She seemed nervous. "I think we should see what's going on in the backyard."

"I agree," Ashley said. We began to walk around the side of the house. Lindsay followed.

"No!" cried Carly.

But it was too late. We turned the corner, and everyone gasped.

Tulips!

Rows and rows of beautiful tulips. Was Carly secretly growing them for the Flower Festival?

7

THE PERFECT GIFTS

"**W**hy are you growing tulips?" Lindsay cried.

Carly hung her head. "I'm going to enter the tulip contest at the Flower Festival."

Lindsay stared at her in amazement.

"Why didn't you tell anyone?" Ashley asked.

"I didn't know if I could do it," Carly admitted.

"She's never grown tulips before," said a boy a little older than us. I guessed he was Carly's brother.

I stared at Carly's tulips. They were beautiful. They were just as perfect-looking as Lindsay's. Both could be blue-ribbon winners.

"Lindsay said you came by her house and took pictures of her tulips. Why?" I asked Carly.

"Lindsay's tulips have always won. I wanted to see if mine were as good-looking as hers." Carly smiled. "They are, aren't they?"

We nodded.

"Carly," Ashley said, "did you ruin Lindsay's tulips?"

Carly looked shocked. "No way! I would never hurt her flowers. If I win, I want to win fairly."

As we walked back to Lindsay's house, we talked about Carly's surprise tulips. None of us knew if we should believe Carly. But we had no evidence to prove she was lying or to prove she ruined Lindsay's tulips. This case was far from being solved.

When we got back to Lindsay's house, Lindsay ran to check on her pink tulips in the front yard. I was really glad they were still okay.

Lindsay kneeled down and began to pull some weeds. Ashley bent down to help her. I noticed how Lindsay's rainbow barrette sparkled in the sunshine. That's when it hit me.

"I've got it!" I cried. "The barrette is 'a sparkly gift to wear.' Remember? 'A delicate rainbow for the hair.' Do you think it's the second gift for the unicorn?"

Lindsay smiled. "It could be."

"But we still haven't figured out the first part of the riddle," Ashley reminded me.

"I know," I said. I looked around the yard. Maybe something would give me an idea. But nothing in the yard was sweet and powdery and sour.

I spotted the gardener's truck parked in

the driveway. A black-haired boy, a few years older than us, was watching me from the passenger's seat. "Who's that boy?" I asked Lindsay.

"Oh, that's Mike, our gardener's son. He's always here with his father. He's really quiet but nice," Lindsay said.

"Let's go talk to him," I said to Ashley. "Maybe he saw someone near Lindsay's tulips this week."

"Good idea." Ashley followed me to the truck.

Mike looked up when we said hi. He told us he was waiting for his father to finish working.

"Have you seen anyone in the Munros' yard this week who shouldn't have been here?" Ashley asked. She explained about Lindsay's ruined tulips.

Mike thought as he reached forward and opened the glove-compartment door. He pulled out a pack of gum. "Nope." He shook his head. "I saw Nick nosing around, but that was this morning."

"He said he was going to write about the tulips for his mini-mag," I said.

"Have you seen his site?" Mike asked. "All my friends are talking about his unicorn article."

"We know," Ashley said. She was staring into the truck.

I sighed. "Well, that didn't really help," I said to Ashley.

"Actually, it kind of did," she said. She pointed at a small metal container in the crowded glove compartment. "May I see that?" she asked Mike.

"Sure." Mike handed her a tin of lemon drops.

Ashley removed the cover. We stared at the little yellow candies, covered in white powdered sugar.

"'First, offer a tasty treat—something powdered, tart, and sweet,'" Ashley repeated from the poem. "This must be it—lemon drops! We found both gifts for the unicorn!"

She turned back to Mike. "May we have some?"

Mike shrugged. "Sure. Take them all."

Ashley smiled. "Come on, Mary-Kate! Let's go put them by the tree!"

8

A PICTURE SAYS IT ALL

Sunday morning we were all up early. Today was the Flower Festival. Today we would also see if the unicorn had come to take our gifts.

After breakfast we raced to the old oak tree. Last night we had left the sparkly barrette and the lemon drops right beside it. This morning they were gone!

Lindsay and Abby began to shriek. "The unicorn came!"

I wasn't so sure. There was no way to

tell what had happened to the gifts. "We don't know for sure that a unicorn was here," I said.

"But we don't know that one *wasn't*," Abby replied. "I wonder if we'll get to see the unicorn now."

Ashley had that dreamy look in her eyes again. "I sure hope so," she said.

Back at the house Ashley and I sat on the grass and watched as Lindsay watered her pink tulips. The judges were coming that afternoon. Abby went to her room. Mike and his father clipped some bushes nearby.

Ashley pulled her detective notebook out of her backpack. She opened to our page of suspects. "Our first suspect is Carly," she said. "Carly has a motive—she wants her tulips to win the Flower Festival. Plus, she's been in Lindsay's yard, looking at her tulips. There's also Abby, but we have no motive for her, and our only evidence was her dirty feet."

"That's not much," I agreed.

"And our last suspect is a unicorn," Ashley went on. "People have seen one in the area, and we saw a white figure in the flower bed."

"We just don't know that unicorns really exist," I pointed out.

"That's true," Ashley said. "This is a strange case." She swatted at a bee flying near her head. I watched the bee buzz around. It landed on the yellow petals of a daffodil growing next to the tulips.

"Wait!" I jumped up. "Look at all the daffodils!" I pointed to the clumps of bright yellow flowers blooming all around the yard. "All the daffodils are fine."

"So?" Lindsay said.

"So, if an animal—like a unicorn—came and ate your flowers, why would it eat only the tulips and not the daffodils?"

"Bill, the guy at the fruit stand, said that unicorns like tulips," Ashley said.

I shook my head. "Animals don't pick and choose as if they're at a salad bar, do they? I bet when they're hungry, they just eat."

"I don't understand," Lindsay said.

"This means that a *person* destroyed your flowers," I said with a smile.

"No, it doesn't," Mike said from behind us.

We whirled around. "Why not?" I asked.

"Because some animals, such as deer and groundhogs, love to eat tulips but hate to eat daffodils. Maybe unicorns are the same way," he said.

Ashley nodded. "Mary-Kate, we need to keep the unicorn on our list."

At that moment Abby ran out the front door. She waved a piece of paper in her hand. "You won't believe this!" she cried.

We all huddled around her. Ashley gasped. "Is that a real, live unicorn?"

I looked more closely. It was a printout of the newest edition of *Nick's News*. On the front page was a blurry photo of a unicorn! I peered at the white animal. I could make out a single horn and wings.

"It looks real to me," Abby said.

Ashley quickly read Nick's article out loud. "'A unicorn was spotted in the neighborhood Friday night—and it had tulip petals in its mouth. Were they Lindsay Munro's tulips?'"

Lindsay gasped. "What?"

I couldn't take my eyes off the blurry photo. Could it really be a unicorn? I stared at it—and that's when I noticed the tree house in the background of the photo. "Look! This photo was taken right here in the Munros' yard!"

"That means a unicorn really was here!" Lindsay cried. "A unicorn ate my tulips!"

THE CHASE IS ON

9

"**W**ait a minute," said Ashley. "Where did Nick get this photo? And how does he know the unicorn was eating tulips? The photo's too blurry to tell."

"I don't know," I said.

"Well, Nick is sure going to have a lot of people checking out his mini-mag today," Mike said.

"Finally something exciting is happening in this town for him to write about," Lindsay said.

"We just found another suspect!" I cried. "*Nick!*"

Everyone stared at me. "Why is Nick a suspect?" Lindsay asked.

"Nick has a good motive. You said nothing exciting ever happens here. Maybe Nick decided to *make* something happen. Maybe he destroyed your tulips and then made up the unicorn story, so people would want to read his mini-mag," I explained.

"And then he could get the most extra credit," Ashley said. She wrote Nick's name and motive down in her detective notebook.

"But what about the unicorn photo?" Lindsay asked. "Doesn't it prove a unicorn did it?"

"Maybe not. Let's go to Nick's house," I said. "I think we need to see the original photo."

Nick's house was not far away. Lindsay stayed behind to tend her flowers. Abby stayed too.

The Martins' house was yellow with white shutters and a wide porch along the front. We walked up to the front door and rang the bell. No answer.

"Look!" Ashley pointed to one side of the porch. We both walked over to a wicker basket. Inside the basket was a pair of gardening gloves and pruning shears—which are used to trim or cut flowers. Yellow tulip petals were scattered on the bottom of the basket.

"Do you think Nick used these shears to cut the tops off Lindsay's tulips?" I asked.

"I don't know," Ashley said. She bent closer to examine the basket.

"Hi!" Nick called.

We both jumped. Nick and his mother stood on the front steps. Nick's mom held a bunch of yellow tulips.

"We thought we heard someone here," his mother said. "We were in the backyard, gardening. Are you as excited as Nick is about the unicorn? He's hoping it will come to our house and eat my tulips next!" She reached for her basket and, with a wave, hurried toward the back of the house.

The petals must have come from his mom's garden, I thought.

Ashley asked Nick about the photograph of the unicorn.

"I didn't take the photo myself," Nick explained. "It appeared really early this morning in my mailbox."

"Who sent it to you?" Ashley asked.

"I don't know," Nick said. "There was no note." He went inside his house and returned a minute later with a large yellow envelope.

Ashley and I examined the envelope. There was nothing written on it. There was no stamp or postage mark either.

"That means that it wasn't sent through the mail. Someone put it in Nick's mailbox," Ashley said.

TOTAL RECALL

A good memory is one of the most important skills a detective can have. Try this activity to see if you are a memory master.

The picture of Mary-Kate and Ashley on the other side of this card is almost the same as the one on the cover. But five things have been changed. Can you spot those five changes?

Answers:

1. Mary-Kate's necklace is missing.

2. The flowers on Ashley's shirt are missing.

3. Mary-Kate's barrette is missing.

4. Ashley's buttons are blue.

5. Mary-Kate's shirt is lavender.

www.mary-kateandashley.com

From
The Case Of The Unicorn Mystery

THE PILOT CODE

Do you want to send a secret password to a friend? Put the word in code! Here's a special code that pilots use when they send radio messages.

What to do: Replace each letter in the secret word with the matching word from the list below.

A–Alfa	H–Hotel	O–Oscar	V–Victor
B–Bravo	I–India	P–Papa	W–Whiskey
C–Charlie	J–Juliet	Q–Quebec	X–Xray
D–Delta	K–Kilo	R–Romeo	Y–Yankee
E–Echo	L–Lima	S–Sierra	Z–Zulu
F–Foxtrot	M–Mike	T–Tango	
G–Golf	N–November	U–Uniform	

Using this code, the word UNICORN would be written like this:

Uniform November India Charlie Oscar Romeo November

www.mary-kateandashley.com

From
The Case Of The Unicorn Mystery

I pulled the photo out of the envelope. It was printed on glossy computer paper. It looked the same as it had in his mini-mag. "This might not be a real unicorn. It could be a fake picture made on a computer," I told Nick. "Maybe someone used a special program to add a horn and wings to a horse."

Nick shrugged. "Maybe."

We turned the photo over. On the back were the typed words: UNICORN. FRIDAY NIGHT. EATING LINDSAY'S TULIPS?

"May we keep this as evidence?" Ashley asked.

"Sure," said Nick. "Let me know if you find out who gave it to me."

"I have one more question," I told Nick. "When we saw you yesterday morning, how did you know that Lindsay's tulips were destroyed? It happened in the middle of the night."

"Lindsay's mom phoned my mom early

in the morning and told her about the tulips. They're good friends. Then my mom told me." Nick smiled. "A good reporter knows how to get information."

"I think Nick was telling the truth," Ashley said as we headed back to Lindsay's house. "I don't think he destroyed Lindsay's tulips."

I nodded. "I wish I knew if this photograph was real. Someone could have taken a picture of the Munros' backyard. Then he or she could have used a computer to fake the unicorn picture and put it all together."

"But why would someone fake a photo of a unicorn?" Ashley asked.

"To make it look like as if a unicorn ate Lindsay's tulips," I said, "so no one would suspect the real culprit. Ashley, I think the person who delivered this photo to Nick is the same person who destroyed the tulips!"

Ashley kept staring at the blurry unicorn. "You're probably right. . . ." she said.

"But unicorns are so beautiful. I hope this photo is real."

I knew my sister was dreaming about seeing a unicorn.

We put the photo into a large evidence bag and tucked it into Ashley's backpack. When we got back to the house, Lindsay was still working on her tulips. They looked beautiful.

"Where is everyone?" I asked.

"Abby's up in her tree house. Mom and Dad went into town. I'm so nervous. I hope I win," Lindsay said.

"Of course you'll—"

"It's coming! It's coming!" Abby suddenly screamed from her tree house.

The three of us ran to the oak tree and looked up.

"Hurry!" Abby yelled. She held a pair of binoculars in one hand. With the other hand she pointed into the distance. "I saw a real unicorn! Out in the meadow!"

Lindsay, Ashley, and I raced out of the yard. Clue, barking loudly, followed us.

We ran through a large field filled with wildflowers. Lindsay led the way. Our feet pounded on the grass as we weaved through some bushes. I was breathing hard now, but I knew we couldn't slow down. If there was really a unicorn, I wanted to see it.

"This way!" Lindsay called.

We raced up a grassy hill. Clue panted alongside us. At the top of the hill Lindsay shaded her eyes with her hands and looked into the distance. Ashley, Clue, and I jogged up alongside her.

"Oh, wow!" Ashley gasped.

I sucked in my breath. Far away in the meadow below was a large white animal.

"It's the unicorn!" Ashley whispered.

For the first time I began to believe that my sister and Lindsay had been right all along. Unicorns were real! "Let's go!" I cried. "Hurry!"

I flew down the hill, my hair blowing behind me, the wind rushing into my face. I could hear Ashley and Lindsay a few steps behind me. Clue was at my heels.

My heart pounded with excitement as we reached the bottom of the hill. Clue barked sharply. I glanced at her and saw a stream ahead of us. Cool mountain water flowed rapidly around small stones. The stream was wide. I looked to my left and to my right. There was no easy way to cross it.

"We have to jump!" I called back to Ashley and Lindsay. I picked up my speed and, with a flying leap, sailed over the stream. Clue leaped over it too.

I kept running. I heard the thud of Lindsay's sneakers as she landed on the other side of the stream.

"Ouch!"

Ashley's scream made me stop and whirl around.

My sister was lying beside the stream!

Sticking Together

Lindsay and I raced to Ashley. She was holding her left ankle. Tears filled her eyes.

"Oh, no! Are you okay?" I asked. "What happened?"

"I landed on a stone and twisted my ankle," Ashley said.

Lindsay kneeled down beside her. "Did you break it?"

Ashley shook her head. "I don't think so, but it hurts."

"Can you stand?" I asked, worried.

"I think so," she said. Slowly we helped Ashley to her feet. She took a few gentle steps. "I can walk, but I can't run," she said. She gazed across the field. The unicorn was a white speck in the distance. "I'll slow you down. You need to go without me."

"No way!" I said. "I'm not leaving you behind."

"You have to," Ashley said. "The unicorn may run off. Go!"

I put an arm around my sister. "You've dreamed about seeing this unicorn, Ashley. You have to come with us." I turned to Lindsay. "You help Ashley on the right, and she can lean on me on the left. We'll go together."

The three of us hobbled across the meadow as fast as we dared to go. Ashley limped slowly, but she never stopped. Clue jogged beside us for a minute. Then she raced ahead, out of sight. I guess we were going too slowly for her.

"I hope the unicorn is still there," Ashley said.

I hoped so too.

Then I heard Clue barking. Sharp, high barks. The way she barks when she finds something.

"Let's try to go faster," Ashley said. She kept most of her weight on her right foot—the one that wasn't hurt. We hurried across the meadow.

I spotted Clue. "Look!" I cried. "Clue found it! She's running in circles around a . . . unicorn!"

We all stared at the big white creature. We moved faster and faster. We were getting close. The white hair on the unicorn's strong body glistened in the sun. I looked up at its face and sucked in my breath.

There was no horn. There were no wings.

We were wrong.

It wasn't a unicorn.

"It's just a horse," Ashley and Lindsay said at the same time.

I watched the white horse eating grass in the meadow. The horse was the only animal around. I shook my head. "Ashley, you had *me* believing there really was a unicorn!" I laughed. "I almost started to believe it was a unicorn who destroyed the tulips!"

"I guess it was a pretty silly idea, wasn't it?" Ashley stared at the white horse and sighed. "But it would have been cool if it had been a unicorn."

"You thought my horse was a unicorn?" We all turned to see Carly's big brother sitting under a nearby tree.

"Matt, what are you doing out here?" Lindsay asked him.

"Just giving my horse, Amiga, a rest. We've been riding for a while. Amiga missed me," Matt said. "Carly and I have been at our grandma's place in the city since we saw you yesterday afternoon. We slept over and got back just an hour ago."

I watched Ashley hop over to a nearby tree stump. She sat down and pulled out her detective notebook. She waved me over.

"What's up?" I asked.

"If Carly has been away since yesterday afternoon, then she *couldn't* have faked the photo and left it in Nick's mailbox this morning," Ashley said.

"You're right," I said. "So who did?"

I watched as Ashley crossed Carly off the suspect list. Nick was already crossed off.

"That leaves us with two suspects," Ashley said. "The unicorn and . . . Abby."

"Wait a minute!" I said. I looked back across the meadow. "Why didn't Abby run to find the unicorn with us?"

"I don't know," Ashley said. "With her binoculars, couldn't Abby see that it was really a white horse? Why would she say it was a unicorn?"

"I'm not sure," I said. "Maybe she wanted us to go out to this meadow for some reason. . . ."

"Mary-Kate! Ashley!" Lindsay pointed to her watch. "The Flower Festival judges will be at my house in less than twenty minutes! We need to go back. There's no one at home but Abby."

I looked at Ashley, and Ashley looked at me.

We had both figured out the case.

"Hurry!" I called to Lindsay. "We'll run. Matt can take Ashley on his horse. We need to save your last tulips!"

11

PETAL PROOF

Clue followed Lindsay and me as we raced back to her house.

"I don't understand." Lindsay panted as she ran. "What's going on?"

"Ashley and I are pretty sure we figured out who the culprit is," I said as we leaped back over the stream. "It's not Nick or Carly, and it doesn't seem to be a unicorn."

"Then who is it?" Lindsay asked.

"It's Abby," I said.

"My sister?" Lindsay cried. "No way!

You've made a mistake. It can't be Abby."

I could see that Lindsay was upset. "Just wait," I said. "I think we can prove it."

Matt and Ashley rode past us on Matt's horse. Clue sprinted after them. Lindsay and I ran as fast as we could. We all met in Lindsay's backyard.

I bent over to catch my breath. Ashley slipped down from the saddle. She looked around the yard. "Where's Abby?"

"Maybe in the front yard," I said.

Lindsay and I hurried around to the front yard. Ashley limped behind us.

For a moment I could only stare.

Abby stood in the middle of Lindsay's last batch of tulips—snipping the tops off the flowers with pruning shears! Pink petals fluttered to the ground.

"Stop!" Lindsay screamed.

Abby froze. Her face turned bright red. She was caught.

We all gathered around her. She had

snipped the petals off seven or eight flowers already. But there were still about thirty beautiful ones left.

"Abby!" Lindsay had tears in her eyes. "What are you doing? Was it really *you* who ruined my tulips?"

"Yes," Abby said softly. She stared at the ground. She couldn't look at her sister.

"You wanted us to think a unicorn did it, right?" Ashley asked.

Abby nodded. "You two were the ones who gave me that idea. You told me unicorns love tulips."

"You faked the photo of the unicorn on your computer, didn't you?" I said. "You put the photo in Nick's mailbox early this morning, because you knew he would put it in *Nick's News*."

Abby looked surprised that we had figured that out. "Yes. I used a picture of Matt's white horse and added a horn and wings. Then I pasted it on a photo of our backyard. I thought that would fool every-one."

Ashley stared at the cut tulips. "You had us chase Matt's horse to get us out of the yard."

Abby nodded. "I wanted to be alone to cut up the last tulips. The judges were coming. I had to make sure Lindsay didn't win."

"Why?" Lindsay cried.

"Because you want there to be some room on the awards shelf for you too, right?" Ashley said to Abby.

"Right," Abby said. She turned to her big sister. "You win everything in our family. Every time you enter a contest, you win. I never win. I destroyed your tulips so you wouldn't bring home an award this time."

Lindsay looked shocked. "That was so mean of you! You should have told me how you felt instead."

Abby started to cry. "I'm sorry. I really am!"

Lindsay stared at Abby, and then gave her a hug. "Abby, please don't be jealous. You're good at lots of things, even if you don't have a shelf full of awards."

At that moment we heard two cars pull up the driveway. Lindsay and Abby's parents were there—and so were the Flower Festival judges.

We all looked at the pink tulips. Were there enough for Lindsay to win?

Sunday evening the whole town gathered at the Flower Festival. The center of town was decorated with flowers and little white lights. It looked magical.

"Thank you, Mary-Kate and Ashley," Lindsay said to us.

"You're welcome," I said. The awards ceremony had just finished. We smiled at the blue ribbon pinned to Lindsay's shirt. Her tulips had won first place!

Carly hurried over to us. "I won!" she

cried. "I won first place for my roses and second place for my tulips. I have the greenest thumb in town. And I have more awards than you, Lindsay!"

Lindsay smiled. "That's great, Carly. But I don't want to always be competing with you. We should just have fun."

"Sure," Carly said, with a flip of her hair. "Next year I'm thinking of growing orchids. I know I'm going to win!"

"She never changes," Lindsay said as Carly raced off.

"You can grow better orchids than she can," Abby said suddenly.

We all stared at her.

Abby laughed. "Don't worry. I'm okay with Lindsay winning now. And next year I may enter the Flower Festival myself. I'm going to have a lot of gardening practice."

"Why?" I asked.

"Mom and Dad are making me work for Mike's dad all summer as my punishment,"

Abby said. "I think my thumb will be bright green after that!"

The four of us walked to a booth selling fruit cups. Bill, the man from the fruit stand who had given Ashley the unicorn poem, was scooping strawberries into the cups.

"I have one thing that I wasn't able to figure out," Ashley said to Abby. "If you just *pretended* to see a unicorn, then did *you* take the lemon drops and the barrette from under the tree this morning?"

Abby shook her head. "No, it wasn't me. I couldn't believe those things were gone."

"Then who took them if there wasn't a real unicorn?" I asked.

"Who says there wasn't a real unicorn?" Bill asked. He grinned. "Some of us say there was."

I turned to Ashley. "I think whether or not unicorns are real will always be a mystery to us!"

PSST! Take a sneak peek at

Wish on a Star

www.mary-kateandashley.com

#40 Wish on a Star

Dear Diary:

Today, I got the coolest assignment from Ms. Hong, my social sciences teacher.

MARY-KATE'S DIARY

We're doing a unit on animal behavior— and we get to study and take care of a real live animal!

Each of us has been assigned to a different animal-care place. We have to observe the animal's diet, habits, relationships with other animals nearby—whatever we see. And this is the best part of all: I'm working at Starbright Stables. I get to take care of my very own . . . you guessed it . . . HORSE!

But I'm not taking care of a horse by myself, Diary. Everyone in class is working with a partner. I was really hoping to work with one of my friends, but instead I've been paired up with Mallory Spaulding. I don't know her very well—she's new here. She seems pretty nice so far. At least, that's what I thought.

At the end of class today, I looked around for Mallory. I wanted to talk about the assignment and get to know her better.

After all the other kids cleared out, I finally spotted her over by Ms. Hong's desk, deep in conversation with our teacher. I slowly wandered over to the front of the room. As I did, I couldn't help overhearing what Mallory was saying.

"Do I have to?" Mallory asked. "If you could give me anything else to do. . . . Please, Ms. Hong, couldn't you change it? I'll work with anyone else—"

I inched closer so I could hear better. But Ms. Hong looked up at that moment and caught my eye. My face flamed, and I quickly gazed away.

"Mallory, let's talk more about this in my office," she said.

As Ms. Hong picked up her books, Mallory turned around and saw me standing there.

"Mary-Kate!" Mallory gasped. She blushed and gave me a worried look. Then she turned quickly and followed Ms. Hong out of the room.

I stood there, wondering what was going on. Mallory was clearly very upset.

She definitely didn't want this assignment. But was it because of Starbright Stables?

Or was it because of me?

Five Lucky Grand-Prize Winners!

Enter to Win a Fun Photo Gift Pack!

The New Adventures of Mary-Kate and Ashley
"Win a Fun Photo Gift Pack" Sweepstakes
OFFICIAL RULES:

1. **NO PURCHASE OR PAYMENT NECESSARY TO ENTER OR WIN.**

2. **How to Enter.** To enter, complete the official entry form or hand print your name, address, age, and phone number along with the words "*The New Adventures of Mary-Kate and Ashley* Win A Fun Photo Gift Pack Sweepstakes" on a 3" x 5" card and mail to: "*The New Adventures of Mary-Kate and Ashley* Win A Fun Photo Gift Pack Sweepstakes" c/o HarperEntertainment, Attn: Children's Marketing Department, 10 East 53rd Street, New York, NY 10022. Entries must be received no later than June 28, 2005. Enter as often as you wish, but each entry must be mailed separately. One entry per envelope. Partially completed, illegible, or mechanically reproduced entries will not be accepted. Sponsor is not responsible for lost, late, mutilated, illegible, stolen, postage due, incomplete, or misdirected entries. All entries become the property of Dualstar Entertainment Group, LLC, and will not be returned.

3. **Eligibility.** Sweepstakes are open to all legal residents of the United States (excluding Colorado and Rhode Island), who are between the ages of five and fifteen on June 28, 2005 excluding employees and immediate family members of HarperCollins Publishers, Inc., ("HarperCollins"), Parachute Properties and Parachute Press, Inc., and their respective subsidiaries and affiliates, officers, directors, shareholders, employees, agents, attorneys, and other representatives and their immediate families (individually and collectively, "Parachute"), Dualstar Entertainment Group, LLC, and its subsidiaries, affiliates and related companies, officers, directors, shareholders, employees, agents, attorneys, and other representatives and their immediate families (individually and collectively, "Dualstar"), and their respective parent companies, affiliates, subsidiaries, advertising, promotion and fulfillment agencies, and the persons with whom each of the above are domiciled. All applicable federal, state and local laws and regulations apply. Offer void where prohibited or restricted by law.

4. **Odds of Winning.** Odds of winning depend on the total number of entries received. Approximately 250,000 sweepstakes announcements published. All prizes will be awarded. Winners will be randomly drawn on or about July 15, 2005, by HarperCollins, whose decision is final. Potential winners will be notified by mail and will be required to sign and return an affidavit of eligibility and release of liability within 14 days of notification. Prize won by minors will be awarded to parent or legal guardian who must sign and return all required legal documents. By acceptance of the prize, winners consent to the use of their name, photograph, likeness, and biographical information by HarperCollins, Parachute, Dualstar, and for publicity purposes without further compensation except where prohibited.

5. **Grand-Prize.** Five Grand-Prize Winners will win a fun photo gift pack which includes an instant pocket camera (i-Zone from Polaroid), 9 rolls of i-Zone film, a picture frame, photo album, and a signed photograph of Mary-Kate and Ashley. Approximate retail value is $100 per prize.

6. **Prize Limitations.** Prizes are non-transferable and cannot be sold or redeemed for cash. No cash substitute is available. Any federal, state, or local taxes are the responsibility of the winners. Sponsor may substitute prize of equal or greater value, if necessary, due to availability.

7. **Additional terms:** By participating, entrants agree a) to the official rules and decisions of the judges, which will be final in all respects; and to waive any claim to ambiguity of the official rules and b) to release, discharge, and hold harmless HarperCollins, Parachute, Dualstar, and their respective parent companies, affiliates, subsidiaries, employees and representatives and advertising, promotion and fulfillment agencies from and against any and all liability or damages associated with acceptance, use, or misuse of any prize received or participation in any Sweepstakes-related activity or participation in this Sweepstakes.

8. **Dispute Resolution.** Any dispute arising from this Sweepstakes will be determined according to the laws of the State of New York, without reference to its conflict of law principles, and the entrants consent to the personal jurisdiction of the State and Federal courts located in New York County and agree that such courts have exclusive jurisdiction over all such disputes.

9. **Winner Information.** To obtain the name of the winners, please send your request and a self-addressed stamped envelope (residents of Vermont may omit return postage) to "*The New Adventures of Mary-Kate and Ashley* Win A Fun Photo Gift Pack Sweepstakes" Winner, c/o HarperEntertainment, 10 East 53rd Street, New York, NY 10022 after August 15, 2005, but no later than February 15, 2006.

10. **Sweepstakes Sponsor:** HarperCollins Publishers.